# FANTASTIC 4

## THE DAWN OF DOCTOR DOOM

TWENTIETH CENTURY FOX PRESENTS IN ASSOCIATION WITH MARVEL ENTERPRISES, INC. A 1492/BERND EICHINGER PRODUCTION IN ASSOCIATION WITH CONSTANTIN FILM "FANTASTIC FOUR" IOAN GRUFFUDD JESSICA ALBA CHRIS EVANS MICHAEL CHIKLIS JULIAN McMAHON KERRY WASHINGTON MUSIC BY JOHN OTTMAN MUSIC SUPERVISOR DAVE JORDAN FILM EDITOR WILLIAM HOY, A.C.E. PRODUCTION DESIGNER BILL BOES DIRECTOR OF PHOTOGRAPHY OLIVER WOOD EXECUTIVE PRODUCERS STAN LEE KEVIN FEIGE PRODUCED BY CHRIS COLUMBUS BERND EICHINGER AVI ARAD RALPH WINTER

MARVEL 1492 PICTURES WRITTEN BY MARK FROST AND SIMON KINBERG AND MIKE FRANCE DIRECTED BY TIM STORY

www.fantasticfourmovie.com

Fantastic Four: The Dawn of Doctor Doom



Printed in the U.S.A.



For information address HarperCollins Children's Books, a division of HarperCollins Publishers, 1350 Avenue of the Americas, New York, NY 10019.

Library of Congress catalog card number: 2005921616

www.harperchildrens.com

www.fantastic-four.com

www.marvel.com

1 2 3 4 5 6 7 8 9 10

❖

First Edition

# FANTASTIC 4

## THE DAWN OF DOCTOR DOOM

**Adapted by Judy Katschke**
**Based on the motion picture**
**written by Mark Frost and**
**Simon Kinberg and Michael France**

HarperKidsEntertainment
*An Imprint of* HarperCollins*Publishers*

# 1

The day was finally here.

Astronaut Reed Richards gazed up at the space shuttle, ready for launch. In just minutes he would carry out his lifelong mission—to prove that a storm in space triggered early planetary life.

Ben Grimm was an ace space pilot and Reed's best friend. He looked at the shuttle and shook his head.

"I can't do it," Ben said. "I can't take orders from that wingnut Johnny Storm. Even if he is Sue's brother."

Johnny vroomed over on his motorcycle. He looked more like a surfer dude than a space pilot.

"Captain on the bridge!" Johnny declared.

Ben checked out Johnny's skintight space suit. "Who came up with those seal suits?" he joked.

Sue Storm walked over with a stack of the

space suits. She began handing them out.

"I did," Sue said. "The synthetics act as a second skin—"

"—that keep the hot side hot and the cool side cool," Johnny cut in.

"I've been working on a formula for that," Reed said.

"Great minds think alike," Sue said. "I guess some minds think faster than others."

*Ouch!* Reed knew his ex-girlfriend was mad at him. Years ago he had walked out on Sue. And Sue walked into the arms of Victor Von Doom.

Victor and Reed were old school rivals. Reed

became an astronaut. Victor became the powerful owner of Von Doom Industries. He had his own space shuttle, space station, and tons of money invested in Reed's mission.

Victor walked over with his director of communications, Leonard. His flashy space suit almost made Reed dizzy.

"This suit will look great on camera," Victor said.

"Camera?" Ben asked.

"The press is ready for you, sir," Leonard said.

"Showtime!" Victor announced. He swaggered to the press area and began his speech: "Today we

stand on the edge of a new frontier. In outer space we will find the secrets to inner space. The key to unlocking our genetic code lies in a cosmic storm. . . ."

"Wasn't that your speech, Reed?" Ben whispered.

Reed nodded. Victor had a way of hogging the spotlight.

Suddenly Ben spotted his fiancée, Debbie, in the crowd. He ran over and gave her a kiss.

"Get back soon," Debbie said.

Ben glanced at the ring on her finger. "Soon as I'm back," he said. "I'll trade that in for a bigger rock."

Victor continued talking. A film of a cosmic cloud played on the monitor behind him. The same type of cloud would soon pass through space. Thanks to special space shields that Reed designed, the crew would be up close and personal with the cloud. And safe.

Reed, Sue, Ben, and Johnny filed into the shuttle. Thrusters were fired. Smoke billowed across the launchpad.

"Now if you'll excuse me," Victor told the reporters. "History awaits."

Victor joined the crew inside the shuttle. The countdown began. The shuttle lifted off the launchpad—and rocketed toward outer space.

# 2

After a smooth cruise phase, the shuttle touched down on Victor's space station. The crew gathered on the observation deck. According to Reed's calculations, the cosmic storm wasn't due for another four hours.

"If you behave next time, Ben," Johnny joked, "you can ride up front with the adults."

"Tell me, Johnny," Ben said. "What do you want to be *if* you grow up?"

Reed and Sue gazed out into space.

"Long way from the planetarium, isn't it?" Sue asked.

Reed smiled. He and Sue had had many dates at the planetarium. But that seemed like light-years away.

Reed snapped out of his warm, fuzzy daydream.

"Are my shielding panels installed?" he asked.

Sue nodded. "Once the doors are sealed we'll be completely protected from the cloud's radiation."

Johnny began unloading plant samples into the air lock. The boxes would be placed outside in the path of the cloud.

Ben got ready for his space walk. He pulled on his boots and helmet. Then he gave Johnny a thumbs-up. Johnny opened the air lock door and Ben stepped into space.

At a nearby control panel Reed checked his data. Something about the numbers didn't click.

According to the readout, the cosmic storm was only ten minutes away!

"No," Reed said, shaking his head. "It's . . . impossible."

Meanwhile, on the observation deck, Victor stood alone with Sue. "Sue," he said, "every man dreams that he'll meet a woman he can give the world to."

*Uh-oh,* Sue thought. *Where is he going with this?*

Victor flipped open a tiny box: Inside was a diamond engagement ring.

"I have four little words that will change our lives forever," Victor said. "Will you marry—"

The door slammed open.

Reed rushed into the room.

"My numbers were wrong!" Reed shouted. "We've got minutes before the cloud hits. Not hours!"

# 3

Victor shoved the ring in his pocket. Sue ran to a control panel and punched in numbers. Reed was right. The cloud was coming fast.

Reed raced down to the air lock. Outside, Ben didn't have a clue, until Reed's urgent voice came through on his radio. . . .

"We need you inside!" Reed ordered.

"I'm not done arranging the flower boxes, egghead," Ben said into his radio.

"Trust me. You're done!" Reed said.

Ben glanced back. An angry cosmic cloud was rumbling toward him.

"On my way!" Ben radioed.

"Event threshold in two minutes," an automated voice buzzed.

Running in space wasn't easy for Ben. Especially with a turbulent cloud on his tail.

"You can do it, big guy!" Johnny called.

Victor and Sue watched from the command center. The oncoming cloud made the control panel flicker.

"Reed, get up here so we can close the shields!" Victor barked over the intercom.

"Not until Ben is inside," Reed radioed.

"It's too late," Victor said. He began punching keys. "I'm raising the shields."

"You can't leave Ben out there!" Sue exclaimed.

"Don't be stupid, Sue," Victor said. "You can't help him."

"I can try," Sue said as she dashed out the door.

"Event threshold in thirty seconds," the voice whirred.

Ben was inches from the air lock. Reed slid the door open. Ben grabbed the edges of the doorjamb when—

*Hisssssssss!* A mass of space dust battered Ben's suit with orange pellets.

"Event threshold in ten seconds. Ten . . . nine . . ."

Sue rounded the corner of the air lock.

"Reed! Johnny!" she shouted.

A flaming spark from a control panel hit Johnny. Steam from a blown gasket poured down on Sue.

Reed yanked Ben inside. As the door closed a cloud particle zipped through the narrow gap. It ripped through the back of Ben's space suit.

Victor thought he was safe, until a control panel exploded in his face. He stumbled back. Lights and equipment crashed down around him.

The storm cloud swirled away into space. It left behind a darkened shuttle—and a battered crew.

# 4

"Where . . . am I?" Ben asked.

"We're back on earth in Victor's medical facility," Johnny explained. "We're all in quarantine."

Ben tried to sit up in bed.

"Reed . . . Sue?" he asked.

Reed was out in the hall. He lifted some wilted flowers from a trash can and walked into Sue's room.

Sue was asleep but the TV was on. Victor was giving another press conference. On his perfectly chiseled face was a tiny bandage.

"Danger is always part of discovery," Victor was saying. "Without risk, there's no reward."

Blah, blah, blah!

Reed snapped off the TV. A nurse wheeled in a cart filled with fancy flower arrangements. They were all from Victor.

Reed dropped his flowers in the trash can. How could he compete with Victor?

Back in his room, Johnny was making a speedy recovery. . . .

"Where do we think we're going?" a nurse asked.

Johnny grinned. The nurse was his type. A babe!

"I don't know if you've noticed," Johnny said,

"but the slickest runs in the world are right outside."

Johnny tore open a cardboard box. He pulled out a foldable snowboard. "Luckily Grandma sends care packages," he said.

The nurse popped a thermometer into Johnny's mouth. Her eyes widened as Johnny's temperature climbed way past 98.6 degrees!

"You're hot!" the nurse exclaimed.

"So are you," Johnny joked. He spit out the thermometer and handed it back to the nurse. "Meet me at four-oh-one, top of the run."

As Johnny left, the nurse gawked at the thermometer. Johnny's temperature was 209 degrees!

# 5

Johnny was hot but he felt pretty cool. He had an awesome new snowboard. And he was about to go down the death-defying black diamond run.

His nurse skied over wearing a pink ski suit and goggles. "Stay right on the hill," she advised. "The left is trouble."

The nurse dug her poles into the snow and shoved off. Johnny jumped on his board and took off after her. He didn't see the snow melting behind him.

"You're on fire!" the nurse shouted.

Johnny looked down. Flames were shooting out of his ski gloves and suit.

As Johnny beat the flames his board veered to the left. Fire shot from his body as he tumbled down a deep gorge. Johnny waved his arms as he plummeted toward razor-sharp rocks. Suddenly he stopped falling and hung in midair.

"I'm flying!" Johnny cried.

Johnny swerved his body past the rocks and crash-landed in a deep snowbank. He opened his eyes and gulped. He was trapped under snow and solid ice.

Johnny's body began to heat. The ice melted and Johnny crawled out.

"I'm not just hot!" Johnny cheered. "I'm a human torch!"

# 6

It was late at night. Victor sat in his candlelit office. A table was carefully set for two. But only one person had shown up for the romantic dinner. Himself.

Victor dialed Sue's number. When she didn't pick up he slammed the phone on his desk. It cracked in two.

*Did I do that?* Victor wondered. But he couldn't worry about the phone or his sudden strength. He had to find Sue.

Victor headed for the door. He stopped at a mirror and eyeballed his reflection. A long bluish gray scar was growing out of the tiny bandage.

Victor touched the scar. It glinted and flickered, like metal.

A few floors down, Sue sat in the compound's dining hall. She was having a candlelit dinner with Ben and Reed.

Ben's stomach growled loudly.

"Pardon me," Ben said. "Bad shrimp."

As Ben left the table he glanced down at his stomach. It was jutting out of his shirt!

*Real bad shrimp!* Ben thought.

"I should be going, too, Reed," Sue said. "Victor is expecting me."

"I can tell you guys have a lot of passion," Reed muttered, " . . . for science."

Sue narrowed her eyes. Reed had walked out

on her. So what was his problem?

"You just don't get it, do you, Reed?" Sue asked.

Reed looked at Sue. His mouth dropped open. She was starting to disappear!

"At least Victor is not afraid to fight for what he wants," Sue went on. "And it's nice to be heard and seen for a change."

Seen? All that was left of Sue were her eyes.

"Sue?" Reed asked. "Look . . . down."

Sue's eyes glanced down. Her clothes and watch were floating in the air.

"Reed!" Sue shrieked. "I'm disappearing!"

# 7

An invisible Sue jumped up. A bottle fell off the table. As Reed reached to grab it his arm began to stretch—two feet out of his sleeve! Reed snatched the bottle. Then his arm snapped all the way back to its normal position.

Sue reappeared. She stared at Reed and said, "How weird was that?"

"You guys!" Johnny shouted as he rushed into the dining room. "You're not going to believe what happened!"

Sue gasped as she looked up at Johnny. His fingertips were on fire!

"Flame on . . . flame off!" Johnny said, snapping his fingers. "What's up with that?"

"It has to be the cosmic cloud," Sue said. "It must have changed our DNA."

"Sweet!" Johnny exclaimed.

But Reed had only one thing on his mind. To find Ben. The three raced to Ben's room. Through the locked door they heard banging and moaning noises.

"Ben?" Reed called. "Are you in there?"

"Leave me alone!" Ben shouted.

Reed heard a crash.

"I'm going in," Reed said. He stretched his arm until it was long and thin enough to slip under the door.

"That is so gross," Johnny said.

Reed's arm wiggled behind the door. He felt the doorknob and turned the lock. The door swung open and the three rushed inside.

"Wow," Johnny said as they looked around. There was broken furniture everywhere!

"Where's Ben?" Reed asked.

They ran to a hole in the wall where the window used to be and looked through it. In the light of the streetlamps they saw a huge, craggy creature. It was running away from the building.

"What is that thing?" Johnny asked.

"I think it's Ben," Sue said.

Victor entered the room. The bandage on his face was much bigger now. "What's going on?" he asked.

"Ben had a reaction to the cosmic cloud," Reed

explained. "And he's not the only one."

"Anybody know where the big guy is going?" Johnny asked.

Reed stared out the window and nodded. "Ben is going home," he said.

# 8

Reed was right. Ben had highjacked a Von Doom Industries truck. He rode it over the bridge to his Brooklyn neighborhood—and to Debbie's house. But when Debbie saw Ben, all she could do was scream.

Ben sulked away. He climbed to the top of the Brooklyn Bridge and gazed at the city lights.

"I can't blame her," Ben sighed. "Who could love a monster?"

Ben heard a sob and looked down. A man was climbing over the rail of the bridge. He looked like he was about to jump.

"You think you've got troubles, pal?" Ben asked. "Take a good look at me!"

The man looked at Ben and screamed. As he backed away he fell over the rail.

Ben ran forward. The poor guy was holding onto a beam and hanging over traffic.

"Grab my hand!" Ben called.

As Ben leaned over, his hulking body bent the beam. The man lost his grip and fell to the roadway below. A tractor-trailer was barreling in his direction.

Ben dropped to the street. He swept the man out of the way—just in time.

But the trouble wasn't over.

When the truck driver saw Ben he slammed on his brakes. The truck swerved and crashed into a steel beam. Soon all the cars and trucks were swerving and slamming into one another on the bridge.

*This is all my fault!* Ben thought.

He lumbered helplessly between the smashed-up vehicles. Suddenly he noticed a burning tow truck. The driver was hurt and trapped inside.

Ben ripped the door off the burning truck. He reached inside and lifted the driver out. Suddenly he was surrounded by a dozen police cars. Officers poured out of their squad cars. They pointed their rifles at Ben.

"Freeze! Put the man down!"

Ben's heart sank inside his big rocky chest. Debbie wasn't the only one who thought he was a monster.

The whole city of New York thought so, too!

# 9

Reed, Sue, and Johnny ran onto the bridge. An officer stepped in front of them with a gun.

"No one on the bridge," he said. "It's being evacuated."

Reed stared at the gun. He knew the officer was just doing his job—but it was *Reed's* job to help Ben.

Suddenly Reed had a plan. He turned to Sue and gave her a wink.

"The disappearing act," Sue whispered. "Right!"

Sue took a deep breath and shut her eyes. But this time she wouldn't disappear.

"It's not working, Reed," Sue said. "I can't believe I let you talk me into this kind of stuff!"

The angrier Sue got, the more she disappeared. Soon, all that was left of her were her clothes.

"What—?" the officer cried as something grabbed his gun. His jaw dropped as it floated in midair.

Reed and Johnny slipped past the officer. They darted around the burning cars toward Ben.

"Ben?" Reed called. "Are you okay?"

"Okay?" Ben cried. He pointed to his giant rocky body. "Can you explain this?"

Suddenly—*boom*, *boom*, *boom*!

Burning cars exploded one by one. A ball of flames hurdled straight at Sue. She lifted her hands to cover her invisible face. The air rippled around them—as if they were surrounded by invisible force fields.

Sue pushed the blast all the way down the bridge. It hit an oncoming fire truck. The truck swerved across the bridge, crashed through the guardrail and dangled hundreds of feet above the water.

Ben grabbed the truck just as it was about to drop. But the weight was too extreme, even for someone his size.

*"Arrrrgh!"* Ben grunted. He pulled the truck over the rail, inch by inch. Soon the truck was safely on the bridge.

The firefighters scrambled out. They were safe but Ben was not. The squad cars were surrounding him once again.

Ben heaved a sigh. He was about to surrender when a firefighter began to applaud. Others joined in. Soon the whole crowd on the bridge was cheering for Ben. He wasn't a monster anymore, he was a hero!

Ben smiled at the cheering people. Suddenly he saw Debbie. But as Ben stepped forward she ran into the crowd.

Something on the pavement sparkled. Ben looked closer and frowned. It was Debbie's engagement ring. She had left him for good.

Reed, Johnny, and Sue gathered around Ben.

"I swear to you," Reed said. "I will do everything in my power until you are Ben again."

"Excuse me!" the fire chief called. "There are some folks who want to talk to you."

Reed turned. He saw a mob of reporters.

"No thanks," Reed said. "We're scientists, not celebrities."

"Try superheroes," the fire chief said. "They're all calling you the *Fantastic Four*!"

# 10

"Fantastic Four?" Johnny exclaimed. "Cool!"

But Reed, Sue, and Ben didn't want publicity. They just wanted a cure.

"Which one of you is the leader?" the fire chief asked.

Reed reluctantly stepped forward. "During our recent mission to the Von Doom Space Station we were exposed to radioactive energy," he said.

"Forget the science lesson!" a reporter shouted.

"What kind of powers do you have?" another one yelled.

"Powers?" Reed asked.

"The day of the Fantastic Four is dawning," Johnny said with a smile. "First up on the superhero docket is—"

"—to find a cure for our problems," Reed cut in. "No more questions."

Back at the Von Doom compound, Victor wasn't feeling heroic. By now everyone had seen the Fantastic Four on TV.

"Reed's comments on TV killed us," Leonard said. "Nobody wants to put their money into a company that turns its workers into circus freaks."

Victor and Leonard entered the conference room. The bankers sat around a table with their laptop computers. Ned Cecil, the head banker, held up a newspaper. He jabbed at a picture of Ben on the front page.

"You promise a cure-all and come back with this?" Ned demanded. "What are you planning to do about it, Victor?"

"I'll cure them," Victor blurted. "If I can cure those freaks I can cure anyone. What better way to regain the company's standing?"

The bankers shrugged and nodded.

"One week!" Cecil told him. "Or the bank pulls out and you cover your losses."

Victor gripped the table. The laptops flickered and lost power. He stared at his hands and wondered, *Was that a glitch . . . or me?*

# 11

Reed wanted a cure and he wanted it fast. So he took Sue, Johnny, and Ben to the Baxter Building lab for some serious testing.

There Reed and Sue got to work. First, they supersized Ben's weight to six tons. Next, they raised Johnny's temperature to 4,000 degrees Kelvin.

"I can go hotter," Johnny pleaded.

"Any hotter would be supernova," Sue warned.

"Excellent!" Johnny said.

"Johnny, that's the temperature of the sun," Sue explained. "You could set fire to the whole earth and destroy human life as we know it."

"Right," Johnny gulped. "Not so excellent."

Finally it was Sue's turn. Reed examined her through a prism machine. Through it she looked like a rainbow.

"You're bending the light with some kind of force field," Reed said.

"That's what I had on the bridge," Sue said.

"Maybe we can make it happen again," Reed said. "Can you remember your mood at the time?"

"I was angry," Sue said.

"Think of something that makes you angry," Reed urged, "so we can make the force field reappear."

Sue didn't know where to start. Until she remembered the day Reed left her.

*How could he be such a creep?* Sue thought.

Reed watched as Sue's body began to vanish. But when he stepped out from behind the machine—

*Zap!*

A force field shot straight at him.

Reed bent his body all the way to the side like a rubber band. The force shot past him and crashed into a wall of equipment.

*That was close!* Reed thought.

Now if he would just be close to a cure.

Victor wanted a cure, too. But first he had to cure himself.

"Your whole body is changing," his doctor said as he studied Victor's X rays.

"Into what?" Victor demanded.

"Into a metal stronger than titanium or carbon steel," the doctor replied. "And harder than diamonds."

Victor cringed. Was he turning into a freak, too?

"I can't pretend to know what we're dealing with," the doctor admitted. "I'll have to call the Centers for Disease Control—"

Victor grabbed the doctor by the throat.

"Look at me!" Victor growled. "I'm the face of a billion-dollar company. We need to keep this a secret."

The doctor gasped under Victor's steely grip. "But . . . you . . . won't be able to . . . survive!" he squeaked.

"I think I'll get a second opinion," Victor said. Then he jabbed his metallic arm through the doctor's chest.

The doctor was dead. But his words were still alive in Victor's head. . . .

Stronger than titanium or carbon steel? Harder than diamonds?

"Just like the shields built on my space station," Victor muttered. "*Reed's* shields!"

Reed hadn't slept in days. He sat in his lab going over his charts and notes.

"Nothing . . . nothing . . . nothing," Reed mumbled. He slammed his weary head on his desk. Something rolled off and crashed on the floor. It was one of the plant samples. The fall had shattered its glass box.

Reed picked up the plant. Then he smiled and said, "The cloud. Of course!"

In minutes Reed filled six chalkboards with calculations. His rubbery arms were busy scribbling when Sue stepped into the lab.

"What are you doing?" Sue asked.

"I'm recreating the storm using the irradiated plant samples," Reed explained. "Last time I failed to account for the unstable molecules."

Sue sidled close to Reed. She pointed to a cosmic storm raging on his computer.

"Last time we saw that, things didn't work out so well." Sue sighed.

"I can't make that mistake again," Reed said.

Reed and Sue had no clue they were being watched. Victor's hidden cameras were spying on the whole building.

"Is Reed any closer to a cure?" Leonard asked.

Victor leaned back as he watched the video monitor. He toyed with the diamond ring in his hand.

"The only thing he's closer to is Sue," Victor said.

"Three days till the bank pulls out their money," Leonard said.

Victor picked at his scar as he watched the monitors. His skin was beginning to peel off. Glinting underneath was cold, hard metal.

# 12

Victor hated what was happening to him, but Johnny was taking his powers to the max!

"Welcome to the ESPN Moto X Games," an announcer boomed across the loudspeaker. "Today, a special treat. Johnny Storm of the Fantastic Four!"

Johnny zoomed out on his bike. The crowd at the race park went wild as he did a series of death-defying flips. A trail of flames shot out of his back.

Johnny tried a complete flip but lost his grip. The bike crashed to the ground and a blazing Johnny sailed right toward the crowd.

Frantically Johnny waved his arms. His burning body stopped in midair—inches away from the stands.

"I'm flying!" Johnny cheered.

He fell to the ground but jumped up to a

standing ovation. In seconds he was surrounded by excited reporters.

"What are your superhero names?" a reporter asked.

"I go by the Human Torch!" Johnny said. "My sister is the Invisible Woman. Reed Richards is Mr. Fantastic."

"What about that giant thing?" another reporter asked.

"He's just the Thing," Johnny said. "We would have called him Rocky Road, but that name is already taken."

The reporters all laughed. But later, Reed, Ben, and Sue weren't laughing.

"Johnny, you have to stay out of sight until

we're normal again!" Reed said.

"What if some of us don't want to be normal again?" Johnny argued. "We didn't all turn into monsters like—"

Ben bristled.

Did Johnny just call him a monster?

Johnny hurled a fireball at Ben. It hit him square in the face.

"That's it," Ben growled. He charged like a bull toward Johnny. Reed stepped in the way of Ben's fist. It slammed through his rubbery chest and landed on Johnny. The punch sent him flying off his feet.

"You want to fly?" Ben joked. "Then fly!"

The reporters had a field day as fists and fireballs flew. Nothing about the Fantastic Four was a secret anymore.

"You call that cured?" Ned Cecil snapped. He pointed to Ben and Johnny on TV. "They don't look too cured to me!"

Victor sat quietly in the Von Doom conference room. He had a feeling he knew what was coming. . . .

"That's it," Ned said. "We're pulling out our money!"

Victor watched as the bankers left the room.

*They may be finished with me,* Victor thought, *but I'm not finished with them.*

Victor slinked down to the garage. He spied from the shadows as Ned neared his fancy sports car. When Victor stepped out, Ned jumped.

"Hey, it could be worse," Ned chuckled. "You could be one of those Fantastic Freaks."

Victor felt electricity surge through his body.

He waited until Ned grabbed the car door. Then he slammed his hand on the hood.

Ned screamed as a charge of electricity crackled through the car—and through him. Within seconds the banker was dead.

"Fantastic Four?" Victor said. "There were *five*!"

# 13

Victor's evil powers were growing. And with Sue spending more and more time with Reed, so was his rage.

"The shields are the only thing that can withstand the energy storm," Reed explained in his lab. "I'll heat up the storm, reverse the polarity, extract the radiation, and reverse the mutation."

Victor tried to hide his anger as he asked, "When will the chamber be ready?"

"In three or four weeks," Reed said. "We have to be sure the storm is stable or it could make the four of us worse."

Worse? Victor smiled to himself. His evil plan was falling into place. . . .

"Let's build it," Victor said.

"But—" Reed began to say.

"Think about Ben!" Victor interrupted. "The

faster we build the chamber, the faster we can save his life."

Reed gave the orders to build the chamber. Sue watched as the technicians worked around the clock.

"Don't let Victor push you, Reed," Sue said. "The chamber isn't ready and you know it."

Reed did know. But he had to show Victor he could finally get it right. And later that night, at the planetarium, Reed showed Sue he still loved her by giving her a kiss.

Ben wished he could kiss Debbie. But who was he kidding? As he roamed the city streets he knew it was over.

Not everyone thought Ben was a monster. The little girl whose kitten he saved from a tree didn't think so. And a blind woman named Alicia Masters who couldn't see what Ben looked like didn't either.

But as Ben sat squeezed into a diner booth, he wanted nothing more than his old life back. And his old self.

"Mind if I join you?" a voice asked.

Ben knew that voice anywhere.

"What are you doing here, Vic?" he asked.

"I'm worried about you," Victor lied. "I know what it's like to lose someone you love."

Ben dug his fork into the foot-high stack of pancakes in front of him. "Reed is going to fix me up," he said.

"I hope you're right," Victor said. "If Reed hadn't made that mistake in the first place . . ."

Ben thought about Reed as he chewed on a mouthful of pancakes. Maybe Victor was right. Maybe this *was* all Reed's fault.

# 14

Reed and Sue had so much fun together at the planetarium, they laughed all the way home. When they stepped into the lab and turned on the lights, the laughter stopped. Sitting next to the transformation chamber was Ben. And he looked mad!

"Ben—" Reed started to say.

"You remember my name, do you?" Ben sneered. "Do you happen to remember what you swore to do?"

"The transformation chamber is almost ready," Reed said. "You have to be patient."

"I'm done being patient!" Ben shouted. He poked his finger into Reed's rubbery chest. It left a big, round hole. "You destroyed my life!"

Reed's body flip-flopped as Ben tossed him around. When Ben finally stopped he looked at Reed and said, "Good thing you're flexible enough to watch your back. Because I won't anymore."

Ben lumbered out of the lab. As Sue ran to stop him she bumped into Johnny. He was leaving, too—for the outside world.

"It beats living in a cage like somebody's science project," Johnny said.

Sue tried but she couldn't stop Johnny.

"Go!" Sue called after him. "But if you're going to call yourself Fantastic—try to live up to it!"

While Sue combed the city for Ben, Reed powered up the transformation chamber.

He watched the cosmic storm rage inside. Then he pulled the door open and pushed himself in.

Victor's heart pounded as he spied on his monitor. "Reed is using it on himself!" he said excitedly.

The screen flashed and went blank. Victor looked out the window. The top of the Baxter Building was glowing.

Outside the city lights flickered.

*The transformation chamber!* Sue thought.

She ran back to the Baxter Building. But when she burst into the lab she froze. On the floor of the chamber lay Reed. His body was twisted like a heap of spaghetti.

"What did you do, Reed?" Sue cried. "What did you do?"

# 15

Victor schemed to destroy the Fantastic Four. And first up was the Thing.

"Why did you call me to the lab, Vic?" Ben asked later.

Victor hid his arm behind his back. It sizzled with electricity.

"To help you," Victor lied. "Reed couldn't generate enough power for the transformation chamber. But I can."

Ben stared at the chamber. He would do anything to be his old self again. "Let's do it," he said.

Victor opened the chamber door. Ben stepped inside. The storm around him swirled faster and faster. Lights in the lab flashed and flickered.

Victor grabbed the power generator. Power surged through the chamber. Ben screamed in pain as the storm hit harder. Just as he thought it would never end, the storm died down.

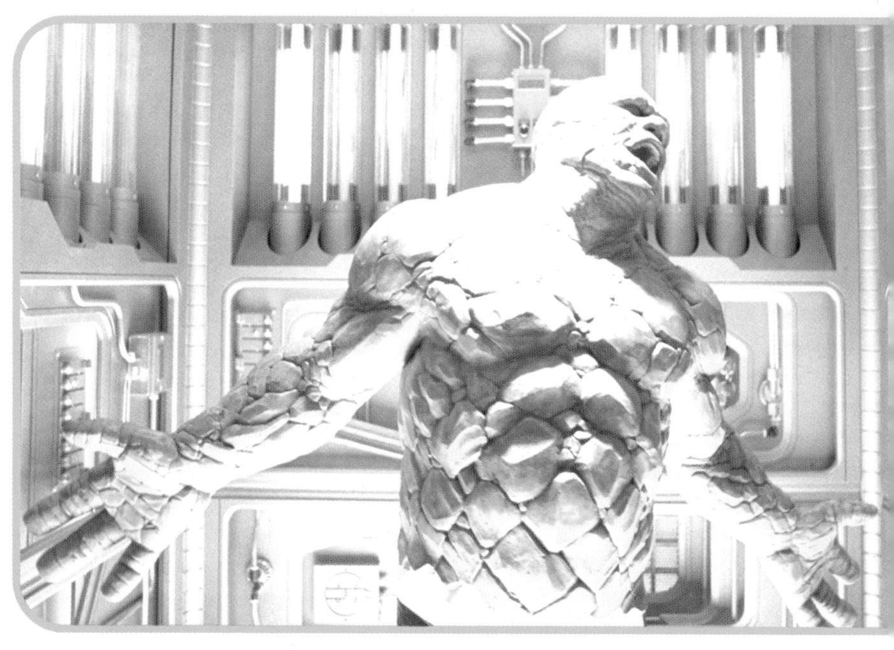

Ben stumbled out as the door slid open. He stared down at his arms and legs. They looked normal!

"Thank you, Vic!" Ben cried. "Vic?"

Ben glanced around the lab. Where was he?

A spark flashed in the corner. Victor stepped out of the shadows. His entire body crackled with electricity. The eyes inside his metallic head were cold and dead.

He wasn't just Victor anymore.

He was Doctor Doom!

"I've always wanted power, Ben," Doctor Doom said. "Now I have an unlimited supply!"

Doctor Doom slammed a steely fist into Ben's jaw. It knocked him across the lab and against the wall. Equipment and controls crashed down, burying him underneath.

"One down, three to go," Doctor Doom said.

Sensing Ben was in trouble, Reed and Sue rushed in; Reed's eyes went wide when he saw Ben. Reed's twisted body had snapped back to normal—but not for long.

"What happens when you superheat rubber, Reed?" Doctor Doom asked. His metallic arm zapped Reed with an electrical bolt. It sent him crashing out the window.

Heat rippled Reed's skin. Doctor Doom grinned as he watched Reed coil down the building like a warped Slinky.

"Victor!" Sue's voice cried. "What happened to you?"

Doctor Doom turned to Sue.

"I'm afraid I'm losing my looks," he said. Then a blast from his arm sent Sue reeling against the wall. Parts of the ceiling collapsed until she was buried alive.

Doctor Doom left the building. He was finished with Ben and Sue. But he wasn't finished with Reed.

# 16

Johnny walked the streets alone.

Not everyone he met in the real world thought his powers were awesome. Some even thought he was nothing but a superheated creep!

A streak of light flashed across the night sky.

*That's got to be from the lab!* Johnny thought.

He ran all the way to the Baxter Building. When he burst into the lab he saw shattered windows and a pile of rubble. A small moan came from the wreckage.

"Sue?" Johnny shouted. He tossed aside chunks of rubble until Sue crawled out. She was bruised, but strong enough to tell Johnny about Victor. "He turned into something horrible," Sue said. "And he's got Reed."

"Flame on!" Johnny declared.

In seconds he lit up like a torch. But over in

Doctor Doom's office, the cool draft was freezing Reed solid.

"Now, what happens to rubber when it's super*cooled*?" Doctor Doom quizzed.

"Why don't you just kill me?" Reed rasped.

Doctor Doom's eyes turned to the window. He could see the Baxter Building, with Johnny blazing in a window.

"Oh, I will," Doctor Doom said. "But first I want you to watch some fireworks."

Doctor Doom reached into a crate and pulled out a flame-following rocket launcher. He aimed it out the window straight at the Baxter Building. Johnny was blazing inside.

"Flame off!" Doctor Doom said with an evil grin.

The blast made Johnny run to the window. He could see the missile heading straight toward him.

"We're superheroes, not scientists," Johnny said. He climbed out of the window and began to fly—fast enough to lead the missile away from the building.

Sue's heart pounded as she watched Johnny from the window. She heard a sound and whirled around. It was the old Ben, inching his way out of the rubble. She didn't know he was there.

"Victor took Reed," Sue said.

"We've got to help him!" Ben said.

"Stay here, Ben. This fight's not for you, not anymore," Sue said. She eyed his body, now back to normal size. He wouldn't be able to help in the fight against Doctor Doom. Sue left the room in pursuit of Reed.

Ben stood alone at the window. He could see Johnny and the trailing missile.

*What have I done?* Ben wondered. *What have I done?*

Sue was right. Without his superhuman size and strength, there was no way he could help.

Ben turned slowly to the transformation chamber.

Unless . . .

# 17

As Johnny flew over the river he knew he had to lose the missile. But how?

Johnny looked down. Floating on the river below was a garbage barge.

*That's it!* Johnny thought.

He hurled a fireball at the barge, and the barge burst into flames. The missile screeched to a stop. It pointed its nose downward and dropped toward the blaze.

"Woo-hoo!" Johnny cheered as the barge exploded.

Mission accomplished!

Across the river, Sue appeared in Doctor Doom's conference room. She saw Reed frozen stiff. Then she saw Victor. The last pieces of skin had fallen off his face.

"Victor," Sue said slowly. "The chamber worked on Ben. It could work on you."

Doctor Doom crackled with electrodes as he came forward. Sue held up her hand. It gave off a small force field.

"Sue, let's not fight." Doctor Doom sighed.

"No, Victor," Sue said. "Let's!"

Sue hurled a massive force field. Doctor Doom broke it up with an electric current.

"Sue," Doctor Doom said. "You're fired."

An electric shockwave zapped Sue. It sent her spiraling through the air. She crash-landed against the wall next to Reed.

"You and Reed always wanted to live together," Doctor Doom sneered. "Now die together."

Doctor Doom's hand clamped around Sue's throat. The other stretched Reed's neck like a rubber band.

"It's my turn now," Doctor Doom growled.

"Wrong, Tin Man!" a voice shouted.

Doctor Doom spun around. A rocky orange creature towered in the doorway. It was Ben—back as the Thing!

# 18

"It's clobberin' time!" Ben growled.

Fists of rock battled fists of steel. The Thing and Doctor Doom broke through the wall of the building and sailed into the air. People screamed as the two creatures fell. They crashed through a glass roof and landed with a splash in a hotel swimming pool.

Doctor Doom ducked Ben's punch. The Thing's rocky fist smashed a hole in the side of the pool. Ben and Doctor Doom rode the waterfall out of the pool and the hotel. Soon Ben and Doctor Doom were battling it out through the streets of New York City.

Ben's next punch landed Doctor Doom in the Metropolitan Museum of Art. Ancient statues shattered as he crashed into them.

Doctor Doom was down for the count, but not for long. He stumbled into the street and yanked a streetlamp out of the sidewalk. Volts of electricity soared into Doctor Doom's body. He was about to hurl the lamp at Ben when Reed reached out and ripped all the circuits out of it. He slugged Doom with earth-shattering impact, knocking him back ten feet.

Doctor Doom stood right back up. "You don't really think you can stop me all alone, do you?" Doctor Doom asked.

"No, I don't," Reed said.

Out of the crowd stepped Reed, Johnny, and Ben. They stood side-by-side next to Sue. The Fantastic Four was united—and ready for action!

# 19

Doctor Doom wasn't worried. "You expect me to tremble at the feet of circus freaks?" he asked.

"I see only one freak here," Johnny said.

"This is who we are," Ben declared. "We can accept it."

Sue shrugged. "And maybe even—"

"—enjoy it!" Reed finished.

Doctor Doom lunged at him, but Reed's arms stretched out with blinding speed, wrapping around and around Doctor Doom's body, squeezing him like a python. "Johnny!" he called. "Supernova. Now!"

Johnny's eyes widened. Supernova meant superhot.

Reed snapped back his arms. Doctor Doom whirled like a spinning top and fell to the ground. Johnny charged over, covered in white-hot flames.

"Flame all the way on!" Johnny shouted.

He exploded into a ball of white light. It heated Doctor Doom and everything around them. Cars melted. Sidewalks rippled. Even the statues in the museum began to crack.

"Think you can keep your rage under control, Sue?" Reed asked with a wink.

Sue nodded. A giant force field left her body. It surrounded the ball of light. As the supernova began to fade, Johnny reappeared and dropped to the ground.

Sue took a deep breath. Suddenly she heard a *thump-thump-thump*ing sound. She thought it was her heart until she turned and saw Doctor Doom.

He was trudging toward the Fantastic Four, dripping with molten metal.

"Is that the best you can do?" He sneered. "You really thought a little heat could stop me?"

"See, Vic, that's your problem. You never studied," Reed said. "Chemistry 101. Last class. What happens when you supercool hot metal?"

Reed twisted on a fire hydrant. His arm morphed into a rubber hose as he sprayed Doom with water. Cold water!

Doctor Doom screamed. Clouds of steam rose from his cooling metal limbs. In seconds Doctor Doom was a cold, hard statue.

Ben carried Doctor Doom's stiff body to Von Doom Headquarters.

Back outside the crowd went wild for the Fantastic Four. They weren't just superheroes—they were superstars.

"I think I can get used to this," Ben said.

But before they could pose for pictures and sign autographs, Mr. Fantastic had something important to do.

Reed reached into his pocket and pulled out a ring.

A diamond ring!

"Sue?" Reed asked. "Will you marry me?"

Sue disappeared.

*Where did she go?* Reed thought.

All of a sudden, Sue's finger appeared inside the ring. "Yes!" she said as the rest of her appeared in Reed's arms.

A smile spread across Ben's stony face.

The crowd cheered as Johnny lit up the sky with a zillion little fireballs. One fireball formed a glowing number four framed in a circle of flames.

It was the end of Doctor Doom.

But for the Fantastic Four—it was just the beginning!